I0453089

ALSO BY KAYVAN

Fictions:

Solutionist v. Satan

The Lord of Persia: Guilty Poet

Nonfictions:

Social Constitution

Political Constitution

Judiciary Constitution

The Verdict of a Nation

Dedication

Dedication

*T*his series is in memory of my father. He taught me, when I was ten years old, that the only difference between the three major religions is their day off: Muslims take Friday, Jews take Saturday, and Christians take Sunday. The rest is the same. They all turn God into their commerce and subject women and minorities to the same injustice. He then held my chin, looked me in the eyes, and said with a grin,

"A word of advice son: work seven days a week."

And this is how I wrote this book, seven days a week.

Los Angeles, Sunday, June 21

Father's Day 2015

K1 PUBLISHING

Presents

Tyrant's Wife

© 2014 By Keyvan D.
Writer Guild of America

All rights reserved.
Published by K1 Publishing.com

Published in the United States of America
First Edition, 2014. Father's Day Edition 2015
Book cover, design, and illustrations, created by Kayvan D.

ISBN-13: 978-0692478141
ISBN-10: 0692478140

This is a work of fiction. Names, characters, businesses, places, events and
incidents are either the products of the author's imagination or used in a
fictitious manner. Any resemblance to actual persons, living or dead, or
actual events is purely coincidental.

FB.com/PersianFire
KayvanD.com
twitter.com/KayvanTweet

Contents

The Personages

The story fuses fact and fiction. Some characters, like the tyrant and his wife, are real-life people, who journey in a fictional plot, while facing a real threat. Others, like the psychic and the maid's daughter, are fictional within a factual story.

The personages come from a wide range of social classes. Some have no education, but have the will to search, analyze and understand, like the nine-year-old daughter of a maid, (in book II) who investigates Muhammad, and discovers that the so-called prophet is nothing but a caravan raider and a pedophile, or the tyrant's wife, who after seventy years of blind obedience, decides to investigate Islam, the religion she was born to follow, and chooses to denounce it, provoking her husband into an irrational reaction.

Preface

The Éruption (series) is a fantasy-fiction exposé that contains observations and revelations, predominantly about sensitive themes that are taboo, and hidden from the public due to their immoral and controversial nature.

These truths have been buried in the cemetery of dogma and political mendacity for thousands of years. In this series, they are exhumed and revitalized through the characters' journeys.

Merci

I am grateful to those friendly faces who work at the two coffee houses where I did most of my writing during the past five years. It was their welcoming hearts; their grace and smiles that made those two shops feel like home. Those baristas were the only angels in a city where love is a mirage, friendship is an illusion, and money matters the most.

ÉRUPTION

BOOK 1

TYRANT'S WIFE

A NOVEL

KAYVAN

Éruption

Chapter I

THE **Bull Rider**

Palace of Niavaran, Tehran, Iran

February 15, 2013, 5:50 AM

At the break of dawn in his immense, dimly lit bedchamber, the white-bearded tyrant of Iran, Ayatollah Ali Khamenei screamed shrilly:

"Aaaahhhhhhhhhhhhh!"

He sat up precipitously in his over-sized bed as if he had received an electric shock and just as abruptly fell silent when he felt wetness on his nose. He touched it, and saw blood on his fingers. The threatening face of the bull rider, and the silver arrow flashed before his mind's eye.

His nightshirt was drenched with cold sweat, and the gold chain he wore around his neck had come undone. Through heavy breathing, he whispered with consternation, "Impossible!" He heard someone in the hallway sneeze, which only traumatized him further and he muttered anxiously, "I'm through!"

Suddenly the double doors opened, and against the yellow light of the hallway he saw the silhouettes of four armed men. They stormed into his bedchamber with their weapons drawn. Still half asleep and shaken by the dream, he stuttered in a cracked voice, "Are…are…y…you…here to….to…arrest me?"

"To *arrest* you?" asked the chief of guards in awe, and immediately switched the light on to identify his boss. With the lights on, he could see that the ayatollah was agitated and daunted.

"No, Your Holiness." replied the chief of guards. "We are at your service, we heard an alarming, pained scream. Is everything all right, Your Holiness?"

The other guards scanned the room with watchful eyes, looking for an intruder and attempted to fan out, but the ayatollah raised his left arm and motioned for them to stop. He swallowed, looked down furtively and then glanced up at them squinting against the bright light. "Turn the light off!" The tyrant's voice had become hollow and coarse, and his eyes were filled with trepidation.

"Your nose is bleeding, Your Holiness." observed the chief of guards. "Shall I summon your physician?"

"No! It's nothing. I had a – I had a bad dream. Everything is okay." Khamenei, realizing the potential humiliation of his situation cried coldly, "Just get out! All of you!"

The chief of guards switched off the light and they silently withdrew as quickly as they had entered.

His mood worsened. The ayatollah heaved a deep sigh, and lay down to stop his bleeding nose. Khamenei's bloodshot eyes stared blankly at the crystal chandelier hanging from the black dome of his four-poster bed, which had a solid wood canopy of black and gold design to resemble the dome of the Al-Aqsa Mosque in Jerusalem.

He wiped his forehead. His breathing remained labored and he could hear the echo of his heartbeat in his pillow, sounding like a war drum. He clutched at his chest and continued to peer at the dome of his bed, which reminded him of the fourteen collapsed domes that had haunted his sleep.

The dream was a clear premonition of a calamity that posed a direct threat to his theocratic throne. Khamenei began muttering an Arabic prayer and slowly recovered his composure enough to think about the nightmare. The ayatollah was troubled and worried. He could not ignore such a prophetic dream.

He waited until his nose had stopped bleeding before sitting up again. Resting his head back against the lushly upholstered headboard, his bulging eyes staring into the emptiness in front of him. He wondered what to do, who to call.

Khamenei glanced at the phone on the nightstand. He did not want to take chances, he was by nature superstitious and a firm believer in theological tales, and he knew that what he had dreamt was a clear omen. He urgently needed answers to his questions and a credible dream interpreter. Only two people could be trusted to share this dream with; one was his henchman, Vahid, and the other was his wife, Khojasteh. Since Vahid was in charge of governmental affairs, sharing a dream with him was neither wise nor appropriate, as any sign of weakness could jeopardize the tyrant's credibility. Khojasteh, on the other hand, possessed a full pampering entourage, and was certain to have a reliable soothsayer among them.

The relationship between Khamenei and his wife had been particularly strained of late. It had been a marriage of convenience – one pursued more for image and politics than for affection. His power, however, was crucial to her, and in that respect, she was very protective of him.

On that morning, no matter how reluctant Khamenei was, Khojasteh was the only trustworthy confidante he could share his forewarning dream with.

He had not spoken to her directly for nearly six months and he had no desire to do so now, but his dream wasn't just a dream. It was a declaration of war. His throne was in danger, the future of his régime was in danger, maybe even his own life was in danger, and Khojasteh was the sole person he could trust. She had proven to be a great refuge in times of vulnerability throughout their married life. The ayatollah stared at his phone skeptically.

The Psychic

Section 12, Evin Prison, Tehran, Iran

*I*n the most desolate and dismal maximum-security prison in continental Asia, locked in terrifying solitary confinement since 1992, was a solicited, powerful and internationally known psychic named Mazdak. A deaf-mute since birth, Mazdak communicated through sign language and notes. His prophecies and dream interpretations were brutally honest and unparalleled in the history of parapsychology.

Lockdown in Evin Section 12 meant spending twenty-four hours a day in an underground, windowless dungeon the size of a double horse trailer.

The only ventilation was through two inches of space beneath the cell's iron door, which also allowed access for cockroaches, spiders, and other insects that traveled between the cells through the narrow streams of watery blood running constantly in the hallway of Section 12.

Mazdak was allowed no contact with the outside world, apart from a few senior régime officials, and the ayatollahs, who would on occasion order him to be blindfolded and transported to their mansions for private family readings. Besides these elites, nobody could visit or consult Mazdak.

Three years after his incarceration, in the face of relentless visitation and liberation requests from organizations across the globe – mainly the International Parapsychology Society (IPS) in New York City, the Human Rights Watch Agency, Amnesty International, and most importantly, his charismatic and tenacious wife, Sima, Mazdak was declared dead by prison officials. Sima called it another lie of the Islamic Republic and vowed revenge.

The Islamic Republic was oblivious to Mazdak's astrological purpose and to his secret—

a forbidden secret discovered by his grandmother, Atussa in 1937, which cost her dearly.

Chapter III

TOWER OF SILENCE

The Aryan Plateau, Proto-Elamite

1600 BC

*A*t the end of the Ice Age, as a result of extensive flooding, the Aryans had migrated from north of the Caspian Sea to the Alborz and Zagros Mountains, and formed what would become the Proto-Elamite. They were the vanguards of Planet Earth's civilization and the founders of the world's first empire: The Elamites.

A thousand years went by. Territorial and supremacy wars were waged, and the division began. The Elamite Empire split up and their descendants became the forebears of three kingdoms: the Parthians, the Persians, and the

Medians. In 600 BC, these kingdoms were in their infancy.

Outside the Aryan Plateau, there were other realms: the Assyrians, Egyptians, Lydians, and Athenians. They were distinct cultures that all followed pagan gods.

Only the Aryans, through the teaching of Zoroaster, practiced monotheism and worshiped Ahuramazda. He had only three rules: good thoughts, good words, good deeds — that was the definition of being a Zoroastrian. Fire was sacred and the temples had perpetual flames burning in them.

Zoroastrians did not cremate their dead, since they believed that the corpses would corrupt the fire. Burial was out of the question since, by their lore, graves were the access to the Underworld and the dominion of Ahriman, the Spirit of Destruction and Lord of the Darkness. The Zoroastrian tradition was to move their dead to Dakhma or the Tower of Silence, erected on the apex of a small hill. The bodies were left on the rooftop of the Tower to feed the birds of the sky, a process that was completed in a matter of hours: the humans' last contribution to nature.

Ahriman had set himself the most enduring mission of overriding Ahuramazda's three rules. He vowed to subdue all humans, particularly women, under his scourge and to purge Planet Earth of mankind altogether. To achieve this, in 1800 BC he developed a toxic elixir, with the poison to paralyze humans' faculty for thinking and understanding for themselves, and put them at the mercy of his agents, who would do the thinking for them. In this way he would gain mastery of the planet in the most vicious way possible, something happened and his first elixir was malpractice.

In retaliation to his second elixir and unbeknownst to Ahriman, Ahuramazda had prepared an antidote, capable of three thousand years of striking back at Ahriman and his agents from the Tower of Silence. Mazdak was the timekeeper of the third and last strike.

———————————

Chapter IV

Tyrant's Wife

Palace of Niavaran, Tehran, Iran

February 15, 2013, 5:58 AM

*A*s Khamenei was considering whether to call his wife or not, again the menacing face of the bull rider flashed before his mind's eye.

He was tormented by what had occurred in his dream and its possible impact on his life. Beyond a shadow of a doubt, he needed a reliable oracle, though he was still reluctant to call his wife. She had a bad side - a dormant shrew that was in her and should not be awakened. Khojasteh was the only person whose wrath intimidated him. She had an ironic and audacious personality. She was self-educated, though strongly superstitious, a woman of no scruples, but a feminist. A social butterfly, yet armed with sharp elbows that could rub anyone the wrong way without her noticing or even if she did, without caring, since she was the most powerful woman in the country. She blindly relied on her amazons the hand-picked members of her female guards, and never trusted any male, not even her own sons.

———

Ayatollah Khamenei, head of the tyrannical Islamic Republic of Iran, known by his sharia title as Guardian Jurist, was a clergyman who had the rash arrogance to proclaim himself the representative of Providence and the most sacred being after God. He cultivated credulity and uprooted education in the minds of his followers. Like a guru to his cultists, he fed his devotees with the bias of religion and polluted their minds with superstitious beliefs in order to establish himself as a divine and indispensable spiritual leader. He masterminded a landscape with a refined system of selfishness, and manipulated his devotees out of all social enjoyments brainwashing them with the Islamic Doctrine, "The only salvation in life is to obey, pay, pray three times a day, and die for Islam if you are called upon."

On June 27, 1981, while Khamenei was leading Friday prayers in a Tehran mosque, a bomb hidden in a tape recorder exploded. Though he lived, the explosion crippled his right arm and hand. That incident changed his destiny, by earning him near-martyr sympathy in the clerical community and boosted his career. It also caused him to develop paranoid schizophrenia and made him feel more connected to his spiritual hero, Adolf Hitler. They both survived a concealed bomb assassination attempt — Hitler in the Wolf's Lair, and Khamenei in the mosque. It persuaded him that Providence had chosen him to finish Hitler's unfinished job.

In June 1989, after the death of Ayatollah Khomeini, the founder of the Islamic Republic of Iran, Khamenei's dream became a reality, and the tables turned in his favor.

At the suggestion of, and influenced by the British Foreign Office, and with the help of his friend and ally, Ayatollah Rafsanjani, Khamenei was proposed to the Islamic Guardian Council of Iran for the position of Guardian Jurist. The Council made their decision based on the similarity of their names and ideologies; both men were equally the incarnation of blind fanaticism, theocratic tyranny, and nepotism toward the clerical community. Both men equally exemplified the very worst aspects of disdain for nationalism and implemented that doctrine rigidly, by sharing the motto, "Islam above Iran." On these grounds, the motion was passed and Khamenei succeeded Khomeini and became Guardian Jurist at the age of fifty. The lavish lifestyle began immediately: million-dollar horses, antique pipes, canes, and living in palaces that once belonged to Persian Kings.

After nearly a quarter of a century in power, he was the absolute despot of Iran. Although the Islamic régime was an obnoxious and newsmaking theocracy, nobody outside Iran knew who the tyrant of Tehran was. The official figure presented by the régime to the world was the president, who had as much power under the Islamic constitution of Iran as a vice president has under the U.S. Constitution.

———————

After eight long minutes of reflection, the tyrant finally reached for his phone on the nightstand and gathering his courage, punched in two digits.

"Khojasteh?" he said anxiously.

A sleepy female voice replied, "Did you fall out of bed, or are you having a heart attack?"

"Don't you jinx my health, woman. I had a dream."

"Hmmm… I think I was having one myself, just before you called. Strange. I dreamt of a big black spider."

"That's it?" he asked impatiently.

"Yeah…. I'm not … I'm not …a…" She yawned and continued, "I'm not good at recalling dreams. Sometimes they come to me throughout the day. Why? What is it? Why are you calling me?"

"I remember my dream in detail, and it terrifies me. I was on —"

"Listen, if this is one of your schizophrenic crises of hearing voices or seeing things, you need to call your shrink and have him change your meds or—"

"Allahu Akbar!" cried the frustrated ayatollah, "I just said I had a dream! I did *not* say I heard voices."

She yawned again and apathetically replied, "First off, you don't need to yell into my ear. It's not even six yet. Second, I need to rest. Today I have my milk bath, the Korean masseuse is on her way, and later I'm having my hair done, plus a facial. Why don't you call me —"

Khamenei stopped her, "Why can't you have sympathy?" His voice was rough with emotion. "I had a *nightmare*. I want to share it with you, and this is what I get after fifty years of marriage? That you have a milk bath while people can't even find milk to feed their starving babies?"

Khojasteh finally sounded awake as she retorted, "Sympathy? I'm sorry, did you just ask for my sympathy after dumping me like yesterday's garbage? Am I supposed to feel sorry for your selfish old ass? And don't you dare lay the nation's deprivation at my doorstep, like you give a shit about starving babies! Whose fault is that anyway? Who's the caliph? Not me. I'm only the caliph's wife. And by the way, it has *not* been fifty years. It's been forty-nine *excruciating years*." Khojasteh recovered her composure, paused, then added, "Why don't you call me around three, between my colorist and my hairdresser, and I will listen to your little dream. Although, after your unjustified and extended silent treatment, I don't know why I should."

The ayatollah, who had been ominously quiet, now growled with fury and yelled, "Listen to me, woman! You are seventy years old with one foot *in the grave* and I—"

She interrupted her husband in a rasping voice, "No, you listen to *me*, you shithead! I'm sixty-seven, not *seventy*, and I will *bury* you and *all your siblings* before I die at the ripe old age of one hundred. Now if you're looking for a fight, you've picked the wrong woman on the wrong morning!"

The ayatollah knew she was wounded and embittered by the separation, but he needed her and couldn't afford to alienate her, so he softened his tone. "Lay off my siblings, I have a much bigger worry. This is an emergency, and I need your help and advice. There's nobody else I can *trust.*"

Khojasteh ignored his reply entirely. "I happen to have a life and I'm entitled to take care of myself—get a facial, a massage, and color my hair." She paused and said more forcefully, "Let me refresh your memory. *You* shut me out. *You* asked first for separate beds, then separate rooms, and now for separate apartments—"

"We're still under the same roof, aren't we?"

"That's beside the point. The point is your demand was insulting and alarming. And now that I'm rejuvenated and have lost weight, you want me back? Together we are-"

"No! No! God, no! I did *not* call for that! You are wrong! Wrong! Wrong!"

She interrupted him sarcastically, "Whoa! Don't hold back your feelings on my account."

"Well —" He tried to play the religion card in an attempt to make her feel guilty. "We are too old to bed together. Allahu Samad! Remember yourself, Khojasteh. Think of your first night in the grave when the Holy Inquisitors, Munkar and Nakir, come to you. What do you plan to answer?"

"I'll tell them to buzz off!"

Khamenei whispered another prayer, then warned, "If you keep on with this blasphemy, I'm not absolutely certain that you'll follow me to heaven."

"Wherever I end up, as long as you aren't there, it wouldn't be hell now, would it?"

Ayatollah Khamenei prayed through a sigh, "Astaghfirullah! Cease being bitter, woman. This is about my dream - which could also affect you." He finally had her attention.

"Me? Why?" She asked more softly, "Was I in your dream?"

"No, but my horse was," replied the ayatollah.

"What's that damn mule have to do with me?" she scolded. "Call me this afternoon!"

"No! No! Wait, wait. Don't hang up!" Khamenei begged. "For delicacy's sake, Khojasteh, are you going to listen, or nag like your mother? If I call you at the crack of dawn, after four months —"

"*Six months!*" She interrupted him.

Khamenei said feebly, "Six months already? Time does fly." He paused, collecting his thoughts and added, "Anyhow…its urgent."

"No, it isn't. It was just *a dream!*"

"It wasn't *just a dream!*" Ayatollah Khamenei retorted, raising his voice "It was a *prophetic* dream. The Quran says that everything that happens to rulers comes to them as a warning via dreams, such as the pharaoh's dream of seven thin cows eating seven fat cows, which was interpreted by Joseph as seven years of good harvest and seven years of drought. Or Nebuchadnezzar's dream of his own statue in silver, brass, gold, clay, and iron, which was interpreted by Daniel as the defeat of Babylon by the Persians, the Greeks, and—"

"Enough with the history lesson! You're giving me a headache. I'm listening, but it had better be a prophetic dream or I'm hanging up."

"It is, Khojasteh, it is," he assured her in a troubled voice. He took a breath and continued, "I was on Zolfaghar, galloping toward a beach. Behind me were fourteen mosque domes, and dozens of three-headed dogs escorted me." He closed his eyes, and tried to concentrate. "By the shore, Zolfaghar stopped, scared of the water, and suddenly—"

"Which one is Zolfaghar, the white one or the black one?"

"What do you mean, *which one is Zolfaghar?*" Ayatollah asked, insulted. "He's a seven million dollar horse, but your question makes him sound like a stray dog. I named him after the sword of our Holy Prophet, who gave it to Imam Ali. That horse is also a saint."

"Was the damn horse white or black?"

"Black."

"Okay, so we have a black horse followed by a pack of three-headed dogs. So far that sounds evil. The horse didn't touch the water, which is also a bad sign. What next?"

Khamenei grew pale and wiped his sweaty forehead. He sighed heavily, then withdrew into a silence that lasted for a few seconds, only to be broken by Khojasteh.

"Hello? I asked what happened next?"

He recovered his concentration and replied, "Zolfaghar stopped by the water and reared up. Out of the clear blue sky, a man in a flying chariot manifested himself. He was tall and dark, well-built, handsome, with a curly, trimmed, dagger-like beard."

"Hmmm…" she said lasciviously. "He should come to *my* dream. How old was he?"

"Young, maybe mid-to late-thirties. He wore splendid armor and held a turquoise banner with a white falcon on it."

"A white falcon banner, huh? Interesting." She paused pensively. "A white falcon banner sounds royal. Did it hold things in its claws, or were they empty? Do you remember?"

He gave this some thought. "Yes! Yes! The falcon's wings were spread, and it carried one sphere on its head and one in each talon."

"What was in them?"

"Nothing! Empty, transparent spheres."

"Transparent spheres? That is bizarre." She yawned and added, "You need a professional soothsayer."

"There was another animal in my dream; a mighty winged bull, with silver hooves, that flapped his wings and pulled the chariot. I still remember the charioteer, his cape billowing behind him and a look of vengeance in his eyes-"

"I don't follow. Was the rider riding the chariot or the wild bull?"

"Both! And it wasn't a wild bull, it was a domesticated winged bull hauling the chariot from the sky into the sea. As they approached the water, as if he had reversed gravity, a giant wave rose up and rushed toward the beach. He landed on the water and he was controlling and commanding the sea and the tsunami."

"Like the Messiah," she whispered, sounding thoughtful.

"What?"

"Don't Christians believe that Jesus walked on water?"

"Yes, but this man was galloping on the water and commanding the sea."

"That's even worse. Maybe the man was Jesus coming back with reinforcements."

Khamenei said in the same harassed voice, "Why would Jesus come after *me*? He was crucified by the Jews."

"Nuances. He was not crucified by the Jews, but by the high priests, and you are the only high priest in today's world who rules a country. You have more power than the popes had at the height of *their* power. You are the caliph of Iran."

"It still doesn't make sense," he insisted. "I'm a Muslim. If the bull rider was the Messiah, he would be going after the Israelis."

"No, he wouldn't go after his own people. He'd go after those who had abused and betrayed them, like Joseph Kaifa and the Romans. In 2013, you're the Kaifa. You were put in power, and have been bolstered by the UK, the US, and France, which are today's version of the Roman Empire."

The ayatollah sighed and said despairingly, "You're not giving me any assurances."

"Well, everything depends on who the banner belonged to and what this rider did to you."

"That is the scary part Khojasteh," he said glumly. "That is the scary part."

Khojasteh sneezed.

Khamenei was alarmed, "God forbid! You sneezed." Terror flashed in his eyes. "The dream will become a reality. I'm finished!"

His fear was contagious and Khojasteh also sounded frightened as she asked, "What did he do to you?"

"Zolfaghar suddenly started to breathe fire like a dragon, the dogs barked at me, the wind flung burning sand into my eyes, and a massive storm crept low over the beach, like all hell had broken loose—a judgment day. While I was struggling with my horse and the barking dogs, a silver arrow pierced the wave and flew directly toward me. I saw it coming at me, and in the blink of an eye, it buried itself right into my throat."

Shaken by the memory, he continued quickly.

"Blood gushed! Zolfaghar shied and reared, throwing me off his back. The three-headed dogs fought to tear at my wounded throat and lap up my blood. The fourteen domes collapsed. The earth opened."

He thought hard, wringing out his memory. "I saw a … a… a precipice, a chasm that led to hell—"

"How do you know the chasm led to hell?"

"It was infinite with inferno fire, and molten lava cascaded from it. In the lava I could see hundred-handed monsters and three-headed dogs—"

"That sure sounds like hell." She paused pensively and then asked, "What next?"

"We fell into the chasm, but I could still see the tsunami reach the shore and wash away everything—me, the domes, the dogs, the horse. The chasm closed, and then all was clear, a white virgin beach replaced everything. The bull rider landed on the beach, descended from his chariot, and planted his banner on the shore. A prayer was inscribed on the white sand in gold dust: *Ahuramazda, protect this country from foe, famine, and falsehood.*"

"*Ahuramazda?*" repeated Khojasteh in a hollow voice.

"Yes," the ayatollah whispered.

"That's a Zoroastrian prayer! It can't be Jesus."

"Maybe he's a Zoroastrian Messiah. Do they even have one?"

They do, actually. He's called Saoshyant, and the Jewish idea of the Messiah is derived from him. Saoshyant is different - more positive than the Muslim, Jewish, and Christian saviors. When their saviors return, they end the world, and people either go to hell or Heaven. When Saoshyant returns, he doesn't end the world; instead, he cleanses it from evil, then renovates and revitalizes it."

"So he's more of a benefactor than a judge or a savior."

"Well…he's like someone who buys a house that's occupied by squatters and infested with rats. He evicts the squatters, exterminates the rats, remodels the house and has good people live in it. Basically, he turns the whole Earth into Heaven. Maybe that's why, after he got rid of you, even dead you saw a clean beach. Assuming he *was* the Zoroastrian Messiah. What is alarming and frightening is that *you*, of all people, had such a dream."

The insulted ayatollah barked, "What do you mean *me of all people?* I happen to run Iran, and I am the most powerful Muslim leader on the planet. If Providence wanted to send a message, it could only be to *me*." Khamenei grew agitated and spoke fast and frantically. "This means régime changes, religion changes, changes in everything, doesn't it? Some sort of questing king is coming, and the damage will be staggering."

"He doesn't sound like a questing king. He acted more like a conquering king, commanding the sea and creating a tsunami. In the end, he killed you, cleared everything, and planted his banner like a tree." Khojasteh paused reflectively. "Come to think of it, that Zoroastrian prayer is what our people are going through right now. They are suffering famine, with hyperinflation and unemployment that is through the roof. Khomeini founded the government on a lie when he said, 'I'm only a clergyman, not a power seeker and do not wish a theocracy.' That lie covered the falsehood, and that doesn't even take into consideration the fact that the IRG turns a blind eye to Afghan drug cartels that flood the nation with cocaine, heroin, and methamphetamine. Young men are too doped-up to rise up against our regime. As for our girls, unemployment, oppression, and poverty funnel them into suicide or prostitution, sometimes as young as twelve. People call us the second Arab invasion, and that makes us the *foe*. So the bull rider is their liberator and he's coming for retribution. I'd say... that would be our cue to start packing."

Khamenei's face grew dark with rage "Would you stop tormenting me! Famine, foe, and falsehood cover the whole planet: America, Asia, Africa, and Europe. Name one nation on Earth where politicians don't lie, and where they don't have a deficit!"

"Maybe that's why it's time for a Messiah to surface."

"Why here in Iran of all places? Why must *our* régime be his first target? And why did you just say we have to pack up over a dream?"

"For two reasons: First, all holy books agree that everything that happens to rulers comes to them as a forewarning via dreams. You yourself just brought up Pharaoh and Nebuchadnezzar's dream. Second, you had a dream that's more explicit than an eviction notice. I don't even know why you need a medium."

"To find out who he is. I have to identify him, find him, and kill him."

"The holy books also say that every time a king or ruler has a prophetic dream like you just had, he never manages to find the savior," she pointed out in a quietly resolute voice. "Moses escaped in his basket, even though the Pharaoh had ordered the killing of all baby boys. The Bible also says that Herod launched the Massacre of the Innocents to find Jesus, and it was fruitless."

"You don't understand, woman. I am running the holiest of all offices. I am God's man on Earth. How can God be against me?"

He picked up his pipe from the nightstand with trembling fingers. It was a rare antique pipe;

its stem was solid gold, encrusted with jewels. He lit it and inhaled smoke, then heard his wife chuckle.

"What?" he demanded.

"That's what my father always used to teach my brothers: 'In order to sell a lie, you must believe it yourself.' I think you now believe your own lies." She continued in a condescending tone, "You are so *conceited!* You are *not* God's man, you're Aunt Maggie's boy. She had Rafsanjani put you into office in the first place - remember? Don't tell me you're suffering a typical politician's amnesia."

He smoked, ignoring the rejoinder, and asked, "What should I do?"

"One thing you can do is find out who the banner belongs to. Other than that, I really don't know how to investigate a dream in real life. One thing strikes me thought."

"What?"

"The black horse – and his name."

"What about him?"

"You said your horse, Zolfaghar, suddenly began to breathe fire?"

"Right after the bull rider appeared."

"Well, maybe he was a catalyst, similar to what lemon juice and heat does to invisible ink."

"What do they do?"

"Think, you fool! They make it visible. Maybe your horse was a fire-breathing demon even before the bull rider appeared, but a dormant one. Like the invisible ink, hidden inside the paper—"

"Waiting for lemon juice and heat to—"

"Took you long enough."

"Took me long enough for what Khojasteh? Where the devil is the connection?"

"Here's the connection. You named your horse after Zolfaghar, which, as you said, was the sword of Islam. It was the sword of the prophet and after him Imam Ali, who played a pivotal part in expanding Islam, especially here in Iran. To the point where Ferdowsi, the most erudite of Persian poets, called Ali 'the butcher of Estakhr.'"

"Estakhr?" asked the confused ayatollah. He thought for a moment, "By Estakhr, Ferdowsi meant a pool of blood."

"No, cluck! Estakhr does mean pool in Parsi, but it is also the name of an ancient town, near Persepolis—'

"Parsi? You mean Farsi?" he asked, exhaling a cloud of smoke.

"It is *Parsi*! As you are well aware, since you speak Arabic fluently, there is no 'p' in the

Arabic language, so they substitute an 'f.' After the Arabs invaded Persia, they also tried to impose their language, though that failed, because the Persians were resistant. However, they managed to infiltrate some words and, as in this case, pronunciations, so now imbeciles like you repeat after them like parrots, convinced it's not 'Parsi', but 'Farsi'. Like they're trying to change the name of the Persian Gulf to the 'Arabian Gulf.' They even have Google rewriting their map!"

"These Saudis own America. The Google thing must be bin Talal," said Khamenei, watching the blue-grey smoke rings from his pipe float into the dome of his bed.

"Who the hell is bin Talal?"

"The same guy who owns the Four Seasons hotels, Citi Bank, Fox TV, and more. He is also a close friend of Eric Schmidt, who happens to run Google. A phone call from bin Talal to Schmidt, and Google publishes falsified information and adds 'Arabian Gulf' to the Persian Gulf."

"Owner of the Four Seasons hotels – that rings a bell." She faltered and added irresolutely, "Wait a minute, is this bin Talal the same guy who sent a million dollar check to the mayor of New

York City after September 11, with a letter of advice that if the US changed its policy toward Palestine, it won't go through an attack like that?"

"Yes, and it wasn't *one* million, it was *ten* million dollars, and to his credit, Giuliani refused bin Talal's offer. Not that I like Giuliani, since he supported the MEK and—"

"Why isn't this bin Talal in Gitmo? The letter and the check are evidence of support, if not financial endorsement of September 11."

"You're not listening, woman! The Saudi régime owns America. They can get away with *anything*. One of the reasons that the Saudis want to remove Assad is because Syria has become the silk road of energy to Europe. The Saudis have planned pipeline projects to Europe that must run through Syria, so they inflamed Syria's civil war through their illegal auxiliaries, Al Qaeda and Al Nusra, in the hope of removing Assad. We want Assad in power just in case the Israelis bomb us, so that we can launch a ground counterattack across their Syrian border. The Russians want to have unique and exclusive pipeline access to Europe, so they back Assad, also there is bad blood between the Russians and the Saudis."

"Why?"

"Because, after the fall of the USSR, in the Caucasus and Chechnya, a fraction of the Muslims were left, and were unbanned, after the communists had banned them. What happened was, those minorities, needed to recruit young people, and they needed funding to expand Islam in Russia, and guess who kicked in?"

"The Saudis? But why should they care?"

"Because the Saudis consider themselves to be the cradle of Islam and they also think all the oil that sleeps under their sand is a gift from God, for them to export Islam and continue the Prophet's assignment. It says on their flag; 'no other God but Allah, no other prophet but Muhammad.' And they depict a sword beneath it, to send the warning message. They have third parties funding groups within Saudi Arabia who promote the growth of Islam, Sunnis of course - all over the world and auxiliaries who fight for them."

"So the Russians are sandwiched between US aid to the Muslims in Afghanistan before the soviet collapse and the Saudi aid to the Caucasus and Chechnya after the collapse?"

"Yes. In fact the other day in our Guardian Council we all agreed, that the US was the best thing that happened to Islam since our

Holy Prophet. First they kicked the Shah out and put us on the map, so that we could establish our Shiite theocracy and Hezbollah. Then, in Afghanistan they helped the Taliban. Two years ago they got rid of Gadhafi with tomahawk missiles to put the radicals in power; and in Egypt they ejected Mubarak and crowned the Muslim Brotherhood. Now the Saudis want the US to remove Assad so they can compete with Russia in gas and oil deliveries to Europe."

"But the Saudis already fooled the US into helping bin Laden in Afghanistan, back in Reagan's time. Why would the Americans be dumb enough to make the same mistake twice? Besides - what's in it for the US?"

"Nothing, the US army is the Saudis' militiamen. Why do you think they went to Iraq?" He answered his own question. "Because the Saudis were worried that after Kuwait and us, they would be next on Saddam's hit list. Also, both of the Bush's ate out of the palm of the Saudis' hand."

"Huh! So much for 'of the people, by the people, for the people.' What do they say? 'Buy the mayor, own the village'? In a movie made back in the 70s, a TV anchor screamed about the

Arabs who owned everything in the US: 'I can't take it anymore—'"

Putting his pipe down on his nightstand, the ayatollah interrupted his wife, "Khojasteh, I don't have time to talk about TV shows."

"It was a movie, Ali. What I don't follow in your flash news, is that I do remember when the Arabs attacked them back in 2001, Hillary Clinton promised that they will go after those who did it and those who aid and comfort the perpetrators. Clearly, with the majority of terrorists being from Saudi Arabia, the ten million dollar bin Talal check, the recommendation of bin Laden to Reagan, plus the current injection of aid to Al Qaeda in Syria, it was obvious the Saudis and Al Qaeda have their heads in the same hay feeder – I'm disappointed in Hillary."

"At that time Hillary was a junior senator who only decorated a chair in the senate, whatever she said, was said to get publicity. Besides which, I just told you the Saudis get away with anything they do to the US, and they own—"

"I heard that already! Stop repeating yourself like a broken record. You're getting Alzheimer's on top of the schizophrenia. Point is female politicians are different to males. We keep our promises; we're not corrupt like you men. If women ran the world, it would be a much cleaner and more peaceful place than it is now. The reason why I'm disappointed in Hillary specifically is because she and I have points in common."

"Really?" In a mocking tone he asked, "What do you have in common with *her*, beside the fact that you're both fake blondes, have nasty personalities and like *all* women have the brain of a guinea pig?"

"Firstly, I'm no longer blonde – I changed my hair color, but of course, since you've been avoiding me and shutting me out for the past six months, you have no clue how I look. For all I know, you may even have forgotten my face. I am *imposed* to see *your* hideous face on every wall of the palace and even when I'm out, on every tall wall of the city."

"Hush, woman!"

"Don't you *dare* hush me! Had I not been in your life with my brain of a *'guinea pig'* you'd still have been a simple mullah, selling namaz in the corner of a mosque and begging for small change, instead of being the Sultan."

"I am not the Caliph or Sultan, I'm only the Guardian Jurist, and humble—"

"Yes, and Putin calls himself president and not Tsar. One thing that you men need to know, changing the saddle doesn't change the donkey."

"Don't you start on me with your feminism! Don't you do that, woman! Not this morning - I had a prophetic dream—"

"Enough with, me, me, me, you selfish old man!" Khojasteh screamed at her husband. "I was talking about myself, and immediately you hush me, because all you care about is *you*. No wonder the world is in disarray. You men are egocentric, warmongering, and corrupt! Just listen to yourself. You want to keep Assad under your wings because you want to be able to finger the Jews with your Hezbollah. Putin wants Assad, because he wants to cock-block the Saudis' pipeline. And the Saudis' auxiliaries kill and decapitate innocent civilians on a daily basis to inflame a civil war, to get rid of Assad, so they can sell more oil. Meanwhile, two million miserable Syrian refugees freeze in tents in the heart of the desert, over you four — four — four *phonies and criminals*!"

She continued with more disdain and in a squeaky voice. "You're all a bunch of selfish, arrogant men, who think only of your own greedy corrupt asses! If women ran the world, wars like that would never start in the first place. Do you know why? Because we women always pay the highest price for war, the Red Army raped two million German females between the ages of seven and seventy, over a period of three years after the war ended. *Two Million!* When war begins, we lose fathers, sons, brothers and husbands. We get raped, over and over and many of us get murdered. Even under the so-called *Holy War* and the Islamic Conquest of Persia women get raped. You men have ego, we women have logic, you men cry for war, we women talk for peace. You—"

"Enough!" screamed the tyrant, "You're giving me a headache. Logic? Women and logic? This isn't even a joke, this is heresy! Firstly, it wasn't 'so-called' it was a Holy War. Secondly, our Holy Prophet considers all women to have been *born* brain damaged. Your feminism is heresy. God forbid that one day women should run the world. I'll strap myself to a missile, and ship myself to the moon."

"Don't let *me* stop you! And take your Arab and Russian friends with you, so all of you can find a way to go to war even on the moon."

The ayatollah let out a sigh of frustration. "Are you through with your hysterical crisis? *This* is why I've had my head in the sand for six months; because you're *bad news.*"

"Bite me!" cried Khojasteh. "I'll tell you what I have in common with Hillary Clinton: we're both married to careless men, who don't listen and don't even care to know what their wives' *hair color is.*"

He heaved another exasperated sigh, "Can you please call a cease fire and stop screaming and sidetracking? I didn't call to learn about the invisible ink and TV shows—"

"I said it was a goddamn movie! See, you're not listening — you *never* listen!"

"I'll listen if you stick to Zolfaghar and my dream, and quit with the distracting irrelevant conversation."

"*You* distracted *me* with your illiteracy and your phony interpretation of Ferdowsi's 'pool of blood.' I was about to say: Estakhr is the name of an ancient town near Persepolis. Imam Ali, the keeper of the Zolfaghar sword, was defeated there and thrown out by its people, so he went back to Arabia and recruited more thugs. He returned and killed every living thing in Estakhr – men, women, children and even their animals."

"Get to the point!"

"Hey! Don't rush me, I'm trying to help you here," Khojasteh scolded. Then she added more calmly, "We also know that Zolfaghar wasn't like any other sword. It was designed with a double point. Why would the Prophet Mohammad make himself a custom sword with two points? What else has a double point and is lethal?"

The ayatollah thought for a moment and replied, "You mean like a killer?"

"No, I mean like a creature."

"A double-barreled shotgun?"

Khojasteh lost her patience and exclaimed in a rattling voice, "You're not listening! I said a *creature*, a living thing, a desert organism that would have inspired him fourteen hundred years ago."

He still couldn't come up with an answer and merely growled. She cried, "A snake, you cluck. A snake!"

"A snake doesn't have two tails or heads."

Khojasteh drew a deep breath and replied slowly, "No, a snake doesn't have two heads, but it does have a forked tongue, doesn't it?"

The ayatollah glanced to his right. Near his coat rack was his precious cane which had a jeweled snakehead with a silver forked tongue on its handle. As he held his chin pensively, he responded, "I doubt that our Holy Prophet would have modeled his sword on a snake. Zolfaghar had double points to take out the eyes of the enemy."

Khojasteh laughed derisively and replied, "Why not use it as a can opener while you're at it?" Her tone became patronizing. "As I've told you at least a hundred times, do *not* insult my intelligence and talk to me like I'm one of your dumb hick followers. I don't think in the midst of the battlefield they would have thought about aiming for the eyes. They were mounted on a camel or a horse, and all their training was for a quick kill. They would have gone for the guts or the neck. We're talking about the Arabs here, the same people who cut off the elephants' trunks in the Battle of al-Qadisiyyah, when they invaded Persia."

"Are you sure they aimed for the trunks? Maybe they were going for the ivory?"

"They were Islamic invaders, not ivory merchants, you dumb cluck! They amputated the elephants' trunks. So they would go berserk and throw things into chaos. They would throw the Persian archers off their backs, and run amuck.

For the Sassanid warriors, it was unheard of, and violated their rules of engagement. They believed that an army must never harm or hurt animals during combat, and they applied this through the ages, from the ancient war against the Assyrians and Egyptians to the Byzantine period."

"I get it. It's almost like using gas in modern warfare. It is prohibited, but Saddam used it on *us* during the war."

"Yes! It's a vicious form of warfare, and it's an Arab thing. This is how the Muslims invaded Persia and defeated the Sassanids. The last thing that Persians heard before they got slaughtered was 'Allahu Akbar'. 1400 years have gone by, and Arabs have not changed. The only difference is, they switched from stealing horses to hijacking airplanes. First thieves, then terrorists."

"Why do you hate them so much?"

"I don't. I'm just stating the obvious and educating you with the historic facts. Can you imagine that someone who uses a sword to amputate an elephant's trunk in battle is going to aim for the eyes? It doesn't make sense. Unless the Prophet used Zolfaghar to torture his prisoners, I don't see why he had a double-pointed sword — it's just not *practical*."

"Suppose the Prophet did model his sword on a snake's tongue. What does this have to do with me and my dream? Unless…you're saying…that Zolfaghar was —"

"The sword of *Satan*!"

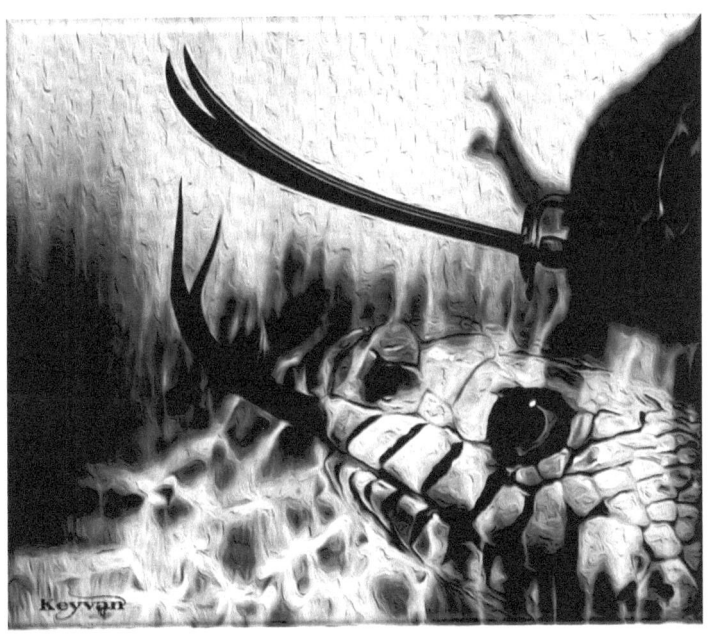

"Astaghfirullah!" warned the ayatollah in a threatening tone. "Measure your words, woman! You're about to commit heresy and —"

"I *am* measuring my words as I will measure my soul in the celestial balance of the Judgment Day." She spoke more slowly, and gently. "Think, Ali — a man who modeled his sword after a snake's tongue can only be a prophet of doom, a devil worshiper. Or he had a forked tongue, deliberately saying one thing and doing another, so his sword was also his tongue. Either way, I instinctively don't trust a man who has a double-pointed sword."

"Bite your tongue woman! Are you saying that you don't trust our Holy Prophet?" cried the outraged ayatollah. He picked up his tasbih from the nightstand and closing his eyes, started to roll the prayer beads between his fingers while reciting Arabic prayers.

Khojasteh said calmly, "Let me finish here. You got me investigating, and now I'm making headway."

"You're headed to *hell!* That's the only place *you're* going."

"*You're* the one who dreamt of falling into the abyss of an inferno, not me. Let me finish. In your dream you rode the black horse that you named after the sword of the Prophet and Imam Ali. You have another horse—"

"I have forty horses."

"Yes, but two of them are your favorites. The other is the white one. What's his name?"

"Zuljinah, I named him after Imam Hussein's horse in the Battle of Karbala. That horse is also a saint."

"Yes, I know. They're *all* saints," Khojasteh replied sarcastically, and asked slowly, "Why weren't you on your white horse in your dream?"

"How should I know? It was a dream. I don't get to pick what's in it."

"Exactly! Dreams are beyond our control. They are either messages to be interpreted, or…" She stopped abruptly.

"Or what?"

She didn't answer immediately. "Suppose…" said Khojasteh, then paused again.

"Suppose what?" he asked impatiently.

"Suppose the memories of our past life come to us —"

"We don't believe in reincarnation in Islam," interrupted the ayatollah firmly, putting down his tasbih and picking up his pipe, which he lit again.

"Well, let's pretend we're *not* Muslim for a second and think of—"

The ayatollah began to cough. "*Pretend?* Woman, what has happened to you? I leave you for six months on your own and you become a whole different person."

"I said *pretend*. I'm talking hypothetically, and I'm trying to help you here." She continued softly, "A soothsayer once told me that dreams can be the memory of our past life."

"What are you insinuating?" the ayatollah demanded.

"Maybe in your past life you went to hell — I'm sorry, I don't mean to make you feel worse, but your dream doesn't sound good, and it *is* very specific and directive."

"Directive…" the Grand Ayatollah mused. "It sure was a directive dream. And that's not all. I woke up screaming in such fear that my guards poured into my room looking for an intruder, and my first thought was that they had come to arrest me!"

"To arrest you?"

"Believe it or not, yes. I was still upset by the nightmare and only half awake. I was confused!"

She chuckled, "How *embarrassing*. Showing weakness to your personal guards and they talk, you know that."

"You don't understand. This dream has a *tangible tail* in my...in my…awakening…in my real life."

"What are you trying to say here?"

"The screaming was not the worst part."

Khojasteh chuckled. "You pissed yourself?"

"No, I did *not*!" replied offended, "My nose was bleeding, and my neck chain had somehow broken."

"What do you mean by 'broken'? Was the chain broken, or had the catch unlocked by itself?"

"It had unlocked by itself."

"You had an intense dream and rolled in the bed."

"It wasn't only intense, it was an omen."

"An omen? I wouldn't go that far. Which one of your necklaces was it anyhow?"

"The one with the name of Imam Ali."

"If that's an omen or a sign, then the bull rider will liberate Iranians from the chain of Islam as represented by your own broken chain."

"I haven't thought of it that way," he swallowed, "but… but come to think of it, you might make sense." He paused and then asked, "Why did you say the bull rider liberated the people from the chain of Islam? They *are* free, aren't they?"

"Free my ass! Let's not kid ourselves."

"To hell with people anyway, they're never happy. This is about me, my dream, and our régime."

"You had a dream with physical evidence: blood and a broken chain, which is beyond theological theory"

"And you're making me feel *worse,* instead of comforting me."

She sighed deeply. "For what it's worth, I understand why you're panicking."

"What should we do?"

Khojasteh paused before adding, "What if God is onto us, Ali? I don't believe in reincarnation but I *do* believe in karma, and karma is a *bitch!* What goes around comes around. Even your idol, Adolf Hitler, shot himself in a bunker. Jack Kennedy ordered the assassination of the Vietnamese president on November 3, 1963 and nineteen days later, he himself was shot. You don't think for a second that we'll get away with everything that we've done to our people for the past thirty-four years, do you?"

"I don't know about Hitler and JFK, but Stalin and Khomeini got away with it, so why not us? We turned Khomeini into a saint and his tomb into a shrine and people go there for their pilgrimage."

"They're not people, they're a bunch of dumb hicks who blow with the wind, and most of them are either basijis or are on the government payroll. Trust me, if your dream comes true, his tomb will become a crime museum."

Color drained from his face. He knew that Khojasteh was an astute woman who was rarely wrong in her assessments. "You're assuming that my dream will come true. Who was the psychic who told you about past life memory? Can he interpret my dream?"

"I thought you don't believe in psychics,"

He exhaled deeply and blew smoke, replying with a shudder, "I need an excellent soothsayer. I need someone like Daniel or Joseph."

"This guy that I know is a psychic who's just like them. He's in prison too. Rafsanjani's wife recommended him, she was very happy with him. She told me he predicted the overthrow of the Shah in 1966, and the Shah, rather than using those thirteen years to save his throne, banned him from his court. Since I'm a scary judge of talent, I didn't want to have him over until I'd investigated him. Word on the street is that these skills run in his family. His grandmother was a famous psychic who was banished from Mohammad Ali Shah Qajar's court. Why don't you call your storm trooper henchman, Vahid? He'll get him for you. I think he's in solitary in Evin."

"Is he the deaf-mute guy?"

"So you know of him?"

"Vaguely. Vahid briefed me about him at some point, about his phenomenon, and something about how the Americans wanted him, but I didn't pay attention at the time. He didn't mention anything about the Shah or the Qajar. Vahid's such an idiot!" He paused and asked, "Did you at least consult him?"

She huffed, annoyed by the question and replied, "Not really. I did, but it was inconclusive."

Khamenei felt she was hiding something. Slowly and suspiciously, he asked, "When and *why* did you consult him?"

"I think it was about five or six years ago, but he wasn't of much use to me. I asked for two things and he turned me down cold on both counts."

"Did he?" he asked, bewildered. "What did you ask for?"

"A birth and a death."

Khamenei's eyebrows rose. He could envision her grinning on the other end of the phone and said, "That's a rather peculiar request. Whose death did you seek, I wonder?"

She laughed at his obvious implication.

He scrambled off his bed and said hurriedly, "Hold that thought, I can't do this over the phone. I'm coming over. I need to look you in the eyes on this one."

"Last thing I need, is a face-to-face with you. Listen, I've given you enough of my time for one day, I think we're done here. Good luck, my consulting services have just closed."

The ayatollah cried out, "I'm on my way!"

He hung up, slipped his feet into his sandals, walked to the coat rack with the cane stand hanger, took off a cloak, swirled it around his shoulders, and grabbed his cane. It was a stunning piece, a walnut cane with a cobra head. The cobra head was an intense amber color, made from a fifty-carat yellow diamond, and its extended neck was covered with rubies and emeralds, which were reflected in the citrine of its yellow gold support. The tongue of the snake was made of white gold. He pressed it down and a long, sharp, shiny blade popped out of the tip of the cane. A devilish fire flashed in his eyes. Smiling strangely, he pressed the snake tongue again and the blade retracted.

He walked toward the door, stopped, walked back to the nightstand where he picked up his pipe and lighter, and then dashed back to the double doors. He opened them to find two bearded bodyguards seated on chairs flanking the doors. They rose and clicked their heels.

"Your Holiness." the guards said simultaneously. He pointed at them.

"Do *not* let the maids in, I'm not up yet."

The guards didn't seem to quite understand, but they replied stolidly, "Yes, Your Holiness."

The tyrant hurried down the hallway toward the wide marble staircase. His bodyguards exchanged intrigued glances.

———

Chapter V

The Prophesy

Section 12, Evin Prison, Tehran, Iran

February 15, 2013, 11:15 am

The automatic iron door of Mazdak's prison cell opened and an IRG (Islamic Revolutionary Guard) sergeant, followed by three privates, entered and jammed themselves into his cell. Mazdak looked at them and grinned with one cheek, baring his two gold teeth.

One of the four IRG men was his personal guard, who Mazdak had taught to sign. Turning toward this man, he signed, "I'm sorry."

"Why?" asked the guard, as the other three watched.

"Because you are still young," replied Mazdak. The color drained from the translator's face as he retreated, already regretting his involvement in the unexpected visit of the Head of State.

"What did he say?" asked the sergeant, as one of his men handcuffed Mazdak and a second placed a hood over his head. Mazdak's translator was still dazed by what had just transpired, but the sergeant asked sharply, "Didn't you hear what I said?"

The translator struggled to regain his composure. In a concerned, cracked voice, he responded, "Brother sergeant, he just predicted that I would die today!" The others laughed, but the translator looked like a condemned man. He added through his teeth to the two other privates, "You don't understand, this guy is not just a psychic, he is *the* psychic. He has been doing this shit since he was four and is *never* wrong!"

"If he were *that* good, he would have predicted his own arrest, you dumbass!" said the sergeant. Then he looked back at the cell.

"What's this?"

The translator ignored this question and said, still agitated, "He *did* know it — he *wanted* to be arrested!"

The sergeant chuckled dryly. "Then he belongs in the nuthouse, not the jailhouse."

Pointing again at the bed, "I asked you, what's this? Why does he have a bed, night table, and books?"

"It took him ten years to get the bed, Brother sergeant, and another five years for the night table and books."

The sergeant pointed at the wall in front of him, "What's that?"

The translator looked back to see a piece of paper on the wall by the sink. "He writes prophecies sometimes."

"Why does he have books, pen and papers? What *is* this? A hotel room?"

"He's a bookworm."

"Only one book should be allowed, and that's the Quran. Everything else ought to be burnt!"

"You should talk to the director, Brother sergeant," responded his guard.

The sergeant yanked the sheet of paper off the wall, and squinting in the dim light, read the prophecy aloud:

"Today is the last day of my last life. I expect an unpleasant visit on this day. Today is the fifth day of the lunar calendar, 1980 years after The Second Man was put to death at age thirty-three.

It is the day of the seven years celestial signal. The year thirteen is an indication that the Third Man's suffering and readiness will comes to its end in seven years, and redemption will be here at last.

He will triumph over his labors that were placed before him in the Land of Thirteen. By the second old moon of year twenty, his third and last personification will venture forth.

The Third Man is the Solutionist. He will walk through the portal of Chamber 58 and cut the serpentine power of Ahriman that stretches itself around the globe and envelops mankind in the chaos of doomsday. He will come not only to rebuild his kingdom that he had built as The First Man, but also to reveal the truth about The Second Man in his second life and what he had really fought for: to abolish the alliance of the foxes and the rats.

Through my deafness, I can hear the trumpets of the final confrontation sounding from the Citadel of the Immortals. I can see the rise of a great empire and the fall of another. I can see the rise of the High Office here on earth. The Solutionist will break the sword of Satan. Iran will be Persia again, and she alone will save the world."

The sergeant looked at the paper pensively and muttered, "'Iran will be Persia again, and she alone will save the world.' What that even means?"

He folded the paper and placed it in his shirt pocket.

'Oh well, he certainly got the unpleasant visit part right." he said with a diabolic smirk, and turned to Mazdak's translator.

"Who the devil is the Solutionist and what's the sword of Satan?"

"Search me!" replied the translator. "I can ask him if you wish."

"Nah! I don't have clearance to interrogate this specific prisoner. Does he make weird prophecies like this often?"

"No, Brother sergeant. This is unusual. It sure sounds like a judgment day prophecy."

"It sure does. What is unusual is His Holiness coming *in person* to Evin to visit a prisoner. That beats the hell out of me," said the sergeant as he reflectively glimpsed at the Allah emblem of the Islamic Republic on his men's uniform, consisting of four crescents and a sword, as if he noticed the sword for the first time, and whispered. "Break the sword of Satan! Hmm." He then pushed Mazdak out of his cell.

"Let's just get the mad oracle up to the director's office."

To be continued…

Please visit KayvanD.com and enter your email address in the author's guestbook to receive information about his' forthcoming books.

AFTERWORD

believe there are three levels of parenthood: the good, the bad, and the terrible. I have to confess that I had a very good father. I wasn't spoiled, like one of my childhood friends who had a walk-in closet filled with toys. I didn't have many toys, but I had a caring father who personally gave me a proper education, guidance, and above all, love.

Three types of crimes can distort the psychological formation of a child for life. The first is sexual abuse. The second is physical abuse. The third is teaching children prejudice and hatred. I have often said that if God were to lift up a chunk of land as big as the state of Texas and drop it on the banks of Gaza, Hamas and the Israelis would still find a reason to kill each other. The perpetual war between them has nothing to do with the size of their lands; they have been brought up, programmed from childhood to hate each other, almost like the Hitler Youth programs trained German children to hate Jews. Parents, who teach their children that one race or nationality is sub-human and savage, mentally contaminate their children and ruin their lives. I recall how my father would always recite a poem by Saadi to me, which has become a motto on the entrance of the United Nations building:

> *"Humans are the organs of the same body,*
> *Created from the same jewelry,*
> *If one organ is harmed, the whole body is in pain,*
> *If you have no sympathy for another's pain,*
> *The name of human you cannot retain."*

In this book I criticize religions for their prejudice, violation of human and women's rights, promotion of ignorance, and above all, for lying. They promote themselves as God's men on Earth, and they are not. In fact, no one is. Anyone who says he is God's messenger is lying.

With regard to my views, I owe them to my father. He taught me, when I was ten years old, that the only difference between the three major religions is their day off: Muslims take Friday, Jews take Saturday, and Christians take Sunday. The rest is the same. They all turn God into their commerce and subject women and minorities to the same injustice. He then held my chin, looked me in the eyes through his spectacles, and said with a grin,

"A word of advice son: work seven days a week." And this is how I wrote this book, seven days a week.

One night during the Revolution in 1979, we were listening to the BBC, as people were doing in most Iranian living rooms. That night, the BBC, who acted as a propaganda machine for Ayatollah Khomeini, broadcast a bit of gossip that, in Tehran, people had seen the image of Khomeini on the face of the moon. We thought it was a joke, but only ten minutes later we began to hear the cries, "Allah Akbar!" We went up to the roof and to our astonishment, people were convinced that they'd seen Khomeini's image on the full moon. They began to scream that it was a miracle and that it validated him as a man of God. My father smirked, looked at the people on their roofs shouting excitedly and then recited a line of poetry from Saadi:

> *"As long as imbeciles are around,*
> *The crooked will cash out."*

In light of all that, this oeuvre is dedicated to my father, who championed the three Zoroastrian rules: good words, good thoughts, good deeds. He married my mother when he was twenty-two, and they were married for seventy years. He was a loyal and respectable husband, an outstanding father, and an honest soldier, as he was a military man. This book is for him, the country he fought for, and the man who founded it: Cyrus the Great.

I hope that the Iranians, who I believe cannot remain naïve perpetually, like those who listened to the BBC and believed Khomeini's image was on the moon, can finally understand that it's not the British or the Russians that they have to blame, nor is it the CIA, SAVAK, or Jimmy Carter; they can't even blame God for presumably turning his back on them. As the Persian dictum says:

"Close your door, and don't tempt your neighbor to steal." My father's message to our fellow Persians was:

"Close the door of ignorance and obscurity, and don't let the exploiters abuse you and impose their puppets on you. Open the window of enlightenment, and be your own master."

It is Islam that Iranians have to blame; it has kept them in the dark for the past fourteen hundred years. The people must release themselves from what Emmanuel Kant called, *"Self-imposed immaturity. Immaturity is the inability to use one's own understanding without the guidance of another."*